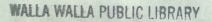

To Pete,
who showed me stars
—*M.M.*

★

For Marijka
—*P.C.*

And so we came forth and once again beheld the stars.
—*Dante*

*S*hhh! Listen. Look.
Right now, night is falling somewhere on this earth.

My House Has Stars

STORY BY
MEGAN McDONALD

PAINTINGS BY
PETER CATALANOTTO

ORCHARD BOOKS • NEW YORK

Thanks to Megan, Cathy, Sandra, and especially Helen and Amelia—P.C.

Orchard Books, 95 Madison Avenue, New York, NY 10016

Manufactured in the United States of America. Printed by Barton Press, Inc. Bound by Horowitz/Rae. The text of this book is set in 15 point Plantin. The illustrations are watercolor paintings reproduced in full color.

1   3   5   7   9   10   8   6   4   2

Library of Congress Cataloging-in-Publication Data. McDonald, Megan. My house has stars / by Megan McDonald ; paintings by Peter Catalanotto. p.   cm. "A Richard Jackson book"—Half t.p. Summary: Young people describe the different kinds of homes they live in around the world—all under the stars.   ISBN 0-531-09529-0. — ISBN 0-531-08879-0 (lib. bdg.)   [1. Dwellings—Fiction. 2. Stars—Fiction.]   I. Catalanotto, Peter, ill.   II. Title.   PZ7.M478419My 1996   [E]—dc20
95-53798

Night is falling somewhere. And now. And now again.
Night is coming to this sky. To houses everywhere.
This house.
 And there are stars.

My house has sharks! And stingrays! Hanging from poles, drying in the sun. My house has the smell of fish and cassava cooking in the pot. When Sonya comes to visit, she rides a jeepney from the city. When I hear "Carmen," I run to meet her. I teach her to walk on stilts around our houseboat.

My house rocks me to sleep at night. I hear the water lapping the sides of our boat, lapping the sides, lapping the sides. So gently I am getting sleepy. When I close one eye and look up through the woven nipa palms of our roof, I see clusters of stars. A cloud-eating shark! One bright star stares back at me like the eye of a fish.

My house has stars!

My house has mountains all around. My house has thick walls of mud. Sheep and goats and even yaks live downstairs in my house. Their heat keeps us warm! My house has only one door. We hang a ram's skull there, to frighten away evil.

Father whispers, "Akam," and nods to me after the baby is asleep. I climb up to the roof to fetch firewood, thinking about the tall tree this wood once was, somewhere far away. The prayer flags flap in the wind, like hands clapping, bringing good luck. I see snow high on the mountains and dream of summer in the tent. Above the jagged mountaintops, I see a sky full of stars. I wish on a star. I wish that someday I will see a tree.

My house has stars.

My house has many huts—one for my father, one for my mother, one for my brother, one for my sister. One for chickens, one for goats, and someday one for me. My house has no corners, just round walls made of mud. So cool inside. My house has pictures on the outside. My mother carved the animals, and I painted them with colored juices from vegetables.

Evening falls and we gather on our knees around the story vine. Bits of china, bone, and hide dangle there. I see a pipe, a feather, the head of a bird. At least a hundred tales are here. So difficult to choose! I point to a piece of python's backbone, and the story begins.

I lean back and close my eyes, rocking back and forth to the beat of the drum, *pum pum*. I dream of the day when I, Abu, will be a drummer like my father. I open my eyes and see stars, like a thousand fireflies.

My house has stars.

My house has paper doors and windows. My house has a bed on the floor. We eat sitting on the floor too. We never wear our shoes inside.

Upstairs in my house we grow silkworms. Trays and trays of silkworms. I sneak up to the attic to feed them mulberry leaves. They glow pale and silvery in the moonlight. I tiptoe across the tatami to look out at the moon, the stars. It gives me the feeling of quiet.

Tonight I will stay by the window and watch the Milky Way. Tonight I say to myself, You must not get sleepy, Mariko. Tonight, the seventh day of the seventh month, Tanabata, the Weaver Princess star, will cross the Bridge of Magpies over the Silver River, to meet another star, Ox Boy. We wrote poems to the stars today, on strips of colored paper, and tied them in the trees. I hear them flutter among the bamboo leaves.

Tonight I see stars. Hundreds of stars. I fix my eye on Lyra, the harp, and Aquila, the oxen. Waiting. Hoping.

My house has stars.

My house has many houses. Many families. My house is made of stones covered with adobe. Our pueblo has many ladders. We go up the ladder and down the ladder to our house.

My house has four eagle feathers, one hidden under each cornerstone. For protection, Grandfather says. Grandfather sang the house-building song and sprinkled cornmeal to show where the walls should go. Then Father built the walls. Mother built the roof with the other women. Our roof goes to Anthony's front door, where he calls, "Hey, Chili!"

My house has a ladder as long as the night. A ladder to the stars. I climb the ladder to watch the night kachina dancers in the plaza. Above them I see stars, like tiny handprints, where Coyote scattered the mica dust and stars were born!

My house has stars.

My house has walls made of sheep's
wool and a real door in the front of
the tent that squeaks like a crybaby.
My sister and I, Oyun, combed the
wool for hours and hours. Mother wet it and pressed it
and hung the wall felts of our yurt. My house has a fire
always burning, and a smoke hole. These walls of wool
were white once. Now they are black from the smoke.
When we move across the desert, we can fit our whole
house on the backs of four camels and two motorcycles,
and carry it with us.

I watch the fire. Sparks rise like stories through the
smoke hole. The sky is dark, a hand over the world. The
hand lifts the sparks up to the heavens, until all I see is
a handful of stars. Flickering. Fading. I move my head
back and forth to make a shooting star across the smoke
hole.

My house has stars.

My house scrapes the sky. It is seventeen stories tall, and I live on the very top floor. From the street below I tilt my head back and try to find the one window that is mine. A soft orange light winks at me. Sergio. My window. My house has an elevator that carries me up, way up to the top.

I tiptoe down the hall and climb the steel stairs through a trapdoor to the roof with my sister. I won't step out to the edge like she does. I lie flat on my back and look straight up. In a world so big, the noise of the city makes me feel small. I could sleep here under the stars. Like city lights blinking in the dark, too many to count.

My house has stars.

O My house has two sisters, six brothers, and me, Mattie. My house has eight dogs and two snowmobiles and miles and miles of ice and snow, white as a gull's feather everywhere you look. Sometimes snow piles right up to the metal roof, and all you can see is our chimney stack! I pull on my sealskin boots, and my brother drives me on the snowmobile to go hooking for tomcods with a bottle cap.

My house has summer where it never gets dark. We pick salmonberries and blueberries on the tundra. I come home to a warm bathtub and the smell of bread always baking.

I stay up late listening to Grandfather tell stories about building an *iglu* or hunting a narwhal or lighting a fire with rocks that look like gold. He says we still live in an *iglu* because *iglu* means house!

In winter my house has darkness all the time. Grandfather teaches me to think small, so I will stay warm, like an animal hibernating. The sky lights up with a night rainbow—streaks of green and red and purple. When the northern lights go out like a candle, my house has stars. Bright stars, like pepper seeds in water, Mother says. White as a walrus tusk, Grandfather says. I say the sky looks like a blue bowl filled with popcorn.

My house has stars.

Our house, the earth.

Our roof, the sky.

Our house has stars.

ALASKA
(Mattie)

AMERICAN SOUTHWEST
(Chili)

BRAZIL
(Sergio)

GHANA
(Abu)

MONGOLIA
(Oyun)

NEPAL
(Akam)

JAPAN
(Mariko)

THE PHILIPPINES
(Carmen)